CHARLIE

and the
Tooth Fairy

CHARLIE

and the
Big Birthday Bash

Hilary McKay

Illustrated by Sam Hearn

Text copyright © Hilary McKay
Illustrations copyright © Sam Hearn

For Henry Steinsburg, with love
From Hilary Mckay

Charlie and the Big Birthday Bash was first published in Great Britain in 2007 by Scholastic Children's Books

To Thomas Cochrane
Thank you for all the good ideas!
From Hilary McKay

Charlie and the Tooth Fairy was first published in Great Britain in 2009 by Scholastic Children's Books

This bind-up published in 2014 by Hodder Children's Books

The rights of Hilary McKay and Sam Hearn to be identified as the Author and Illustrator of the Work respectively have been asserted by them in accordance with the Copyright, Designs and Patents Act 1988

1

A Catalogue record for this book is available from the British Library

ISBN 978 1 444 91925 7

Typeset by Avon DataSet Ltd, Bidford on Avon, Warwickshire
Printed and bound by CPI Group (UK) Ltd, Croydon, CR0 4YY

The paper and board used in this paperback by Hodder Children's Books are natural recyclable products made from wood grown in sustainable forests. The manufacturing processes conform to the environmental regulations of the country of origin.

Hodder Children's Books
a division of Hachette Children's Books
338 Euston Road, London NW1 3BH
An Hachette UK company

CHARLIE

and the

Tooth Fairy

CHARLIE

and the

Big Birthday Bash

Contents

Charlie and the
Tooth Fairy

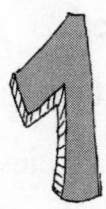

The First Tooth

Charlie had four wobbly teeth.
He had:

One that was rather wobbly.

One that was quite wobbly.

One that was slightly wobbly.

One that was

just beginning to be wobbly.

He had them all together, and he was very excited about it because they were his first wobbly teeth.

Charlie also had a big brother called Max. Max was very clever. He knew things most other people didn't know, like what chewing gum was made of and how magnets worked and the way to tell if strange dogs were friendly or not. Max knew so much and was right so often that it was hardly worth arguing with him.

Whenever Charlie wanted to know something he would go to Max for the answer. And if he wanted to prove to anyone that something was true he would say, 'If you don't believe me, ask Max!'

And then whoever Charlie was talking to would know that it really was true, because everyone knew how clever Max was.

So Max was a very useful brother to Charlie.

But Max was not useful when Charlie discovered that he had four wobbly teeth.

Charlie showed Max his wobbliest tooth, and asked, 'How can I make it come out faster?'

Max looked at the tooth and said, 'You can't. It's not that loose! It might be there for ages yet! Anyway, what's the hurry?'

'I need it for the tooth fairy,' said

Charlie, with his fingers in his mouth, giving his wobbliest tooth an extra wobble. Charlie was very much looking forward to getting his teeth out, one by one, and leaving them under his pillow for the tooth fairy. His best friend, Henry, had told him about her.

'The tooth fairy!' repeated Max. 'The tooth fairy is for kids!'

'For kids?'

'Yes, *and*,' said Max, 'the tooth fairy is a waste of teeth!'

'A waste of teeth?'

'You'll find out!' said Max, walking away.

After Max had gone, Charlie remembered that his brother had always been like this about the tooth fairy. When Max's own teeth had fallen out he had not put them under his pillow. He had hidden them away in a secret place instead.

'Who wants fairies crawling around their bed while they're asleep?' Max had asked. 'And what kind of person sells *their own teeth*?'

Max was no help at all about wobbly teeth, but Charlie's best friend, Henry, was.

Henry was an expert on teeth. Four of his had come out already. He didn't care. He liked the gaps. He had pulled all four out himself, and enjoyed doing it. He thought he might be a dentist one day, just for the pleasure of pulling out teeth.

When Charlie's wobbliest tooth refused to get any more wobbly and it began to look like it really

wouldn't be out for ages (just like Max had said), Henry kindly offered to help speed it up.

'If you're really sure you want it out,' he said.

'Of course I am!'

'Well then,' said Henry. 'You need a method. In fact, you need *The Newly Invented Look At The Lovely View Method.*'

'Do I?'

'Trust me, I'm an expert,' said Henry, and Charlie, who knew that in the matter of teeth Henry really was an expert, said, 'OK.'

Then Henry went home and returned with a reel of dental floss.

'We need to go up to your bedroom,'

he told Charlie.

'Why?'

'So you can look at the lovely view,' said Henry.

Upstairs in Charlie's bedroom, Henry tied a long piece of dental floss to Charlie's tooth.

Then he looked around for something heavy to tie on the other end.

'A rock would be good,' said Henry.

Unfortunately Charlie did not have any rocks in his bedroom, but he did have a quite heavy *Doctor Who* TARDIS.

'It'll have to do,' said Henry, and made the TARDIS very much heavier by stuffing inside three Daleks, Doctor Who, a large bag of marbles and a red London double decker bus. The marbles and the bus were Charlie's idea.

Charlie was just as pleased as Henry to be trying *The Newly Invented Look At The Lovely View Method* of tooth extraction. It had been explained to him very carefully by Henry, cheerful owner of four missing teeth.

Charlie was sure Henry knew what he was doing.

When Henry opened Charlie's bedroom window, he still thought so.

When Henry said, 'Now lean out as far as you can,' Charlie knew it was the right thing to do.

When Henry said, 'Now look at the lovely view!' Charlie looked, and he had just opened his mouth to say, 'It's not that lovely,' when Henry reached behind him, picked up the now enormously heavy TARDIS, said, 'Trust me, I've done this millions of times,' and dropped it out over the window sill.

If Max had not come in at that moment,

seen what was happening and rugby
tackled Charlie from right across the
room, Charlie would have gone out over
the window sill too.

Instead he was pinned to the window
frame by Max, while from his wobbly
tooth swung a TARDIS, three Daleks,
Doctor Who, a bag of marbles and a
London bus.

'AAAARRRRGGGHHH!' roared
Charlie, and then stopped very suddenly
because the TARDIS had gone smashing
to the ground below, and so, attached
to the piece of dental floss, had his first
wobbly tooth.

'It's out!' he cried joyfully, and rushed
downstairs to collect the tooth with
Henry after him.

'What did you think of that?' asked Henry, bouncing with pride. 'Wasn't it cool? Wasn't it great? Did you really nearly fall out of the window?'

'Yes, I did,' said Charlie. 'I felt my feet lift off the ground!'

'Gosh! Actually off the ground?'

'Yes. Promise. If you don't believe me, ask Max! Look at this tooth! It's got blood and everything! And it's loads bigger than I thought it would be. I'm putting it under my pillow tonight.'

There were now three wobbly teeth and a dark bloody hole in Charlie's mouth, and Charlie was very happy. He and Henry showed the tooth to everyone.

'You should keep it for ever,' said Max, but the grown-ups agreed that it was perfect for the tooth fairy.

Henry's mother told Charlie something about the tooth fairy that Charlie had not known before.

'She only comes to tidy bedrooms, you know,' she said.

'What?' asked Charlie, and he looked across at his own mother, who nodded in agreement, and then Henry said, 'It's true. I've had to tidy mine *four times* now. Once for each tooth. And she's really fussy! It takes ages!'

'Told you the tooth fairy was a waste of time,' said Max.

Charlie did not let Max put him off. He tidied his bedroom by kicking all the toys and shoes under the bed, bundling his clothes into the bottom of the wardrobe, and putting his beanbag on top of his homemade fossil-making machine.

'She's really fussy,' his mum reminded him, coming up to see how he was getting on, so Charlie stuffed the clothes in drawers, dropped the shoes over the banister into the hall, carried an armload of toys down to the living room and pushed them behind the sofa, and took the fossil-making machine to Henry's.

Now the bedroom looked much better, and Charlie was exhausted. He put his tooth under his pillow, and went to bed. And in the night the tooth fairy came.

And she left him a brand new, solid-gold-looking, extra shiny one pound coin.

The Second Tooth

'One pound?' said Charlie. '*One pound!* What a cheek! Henry's tooth fairy leaves him two!'

'What?' asked Charlie's mum. 'Two pounds for a tooth! She must be mad! And I don't suppose he puts it in his money box either! I bet he spends it all on sweets.'

'Of course he does,' said Charlie.

'Well then,' said Charlie's mum, as if that was the end of the matter.

'It's not fair,' Charlie complained to Henry, and Henry agreed that he was right.

'One pound!' said Charlie crossly.

'Give it to me if you don't want it,' said his mother.

'Of course I want it!' said Charlie, and went with Henry to the sweet shop on the corner to spend it. They bought pickled onion rings, jelly worms, chalk lollies and bubblegum.

'Disgusting,' said Charlie's mum. 'Next time you have a wobbly tooth I've a good mind to leave the tooth fairy instructions saying fifty pence is plenty.'

Charlie was so surprised to hear that you could leave instructions to the tooth fairy that he allowed the bubble he had just blown to burst all over his face. He thought very hard as he picked it off and chewed it up again.

'I've got an idea,' he told Henry.

'What?' asked Henry, gnawing on a chalk lolly with his back teeth because he hadn't any front ones.

'I'll tell you when I

get my next tooth out.'

'How wobbly is your next tooth?'
asked Henry, interestedly.

'Quite. Getting looser all the time.'

'I am a very big expert on wobbly
teeth,' reminded Henry, helping himself
to the last jelly worm.

'Yes, I know. Give that worm back.'

'I've licked it.'

'Makes no difference. Give it back.'

Henry gave half back and continued,

'There's *The Very Simple Remote Control Method* if you need any help.'

'The what?'

'*Very Simple Remote Control Method.*'

'Does it hurt?'

'Hurt?' asked Henry. 'Hurt? Why would it hurt? Do you want to try it?'

'No,' said Charlie, but the next day, he said, 'I might,' and the day after that he said, 'Perhaps,' and the day after that he said, 'OK.'

'You have made the right decision,' said Henry. 'Trust me. I'm an expert.'

With *The Very Simple Remote Control Method,* the end of the dental floss that was not attached to Charlie's tooth was tied to his remote controlled racing car. This was a fascinating idea to Charlie, especially (as Henry pointed out) as it had the added advantage of putting Charlie in no danger of falling out of the window.

'All done on ground level!' boasted Henry, picking up the handset. 'Admit it can't go wrong!'

It went wrong because of Charlie.

Charlie simply could not bear to stand still while the car drove away with his tooth.

'Don't run after it!' shrieked Henry, nearly dead with laughing, but Charlie could not help running after it.

The faster Henry raced the car round and round the garden, the faster Charlie ran. For a while Henry had a remote

control friend, and he made Charlie
race forward, and skid round corners
and do handbrake turns and sudden
changes of direction, all the time with
his mouth wide open and roaring,
'NOOOOOOOOOO!!!!'

It was the most fun Henry had had
for ages. He would have kept it up all
afternoon if Charlie had not fallen down
on top of the car.

Charlie's racing car lost a wheel,

Charlie himself hurt both his knees, and when he attacked Henry to try and stop him laughing, the aerial on the handset was broken off. It was not until Henry was flat on his stomach with Charlie on top of him stuffing grass down the back of his neck, that Charlie suddenly realized that his mouth felt different.

'My tooth!' he exclaimed, and there it was, jagged and wonderful and still tied to the car.

'My remote control tooth!' said Charlie, dribbling blood as he gloated over it.

'You might say "thank you",' remarked Henry, picking sticks and grass out from the neck of his shirt. 'It would still be stuck in your mouth if it wasn't for me.'

'Oh, well, thank you, I suppose,' said Charlie. 'You might say "sorry" for making me break my car.'

'If you like,' agreed Henry. 'Sorry, then. But I expect Max will be able to mend it.'

'Not the aerial,' said Charlie. 'We've

broken them before. They don't mend; you have to buy new ones. They cost about a million pounds!'

'A million pounds!' repeated Henry, scornfully. 'They don't!'

'Yes, they do. If you don't believe me, ask Max!'

'I will,' said Henry, and went with Charlie when he took the car inside.

Charlie showed Max the new bloody hole in his mouth beside the old bloody hole in his mouth, his two remaining wobbly teeth, and the broken car.

Max admired the holes, wobbled

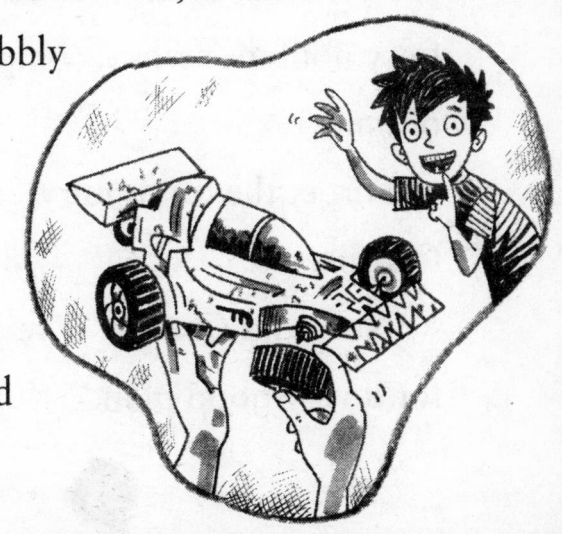

the teeth, and looked carefully at the car. The wheel could be mended no problem, he said, but the handset would need a new aerial, which would cost about a million pounds.

'Still, it got my tooth out!' said Charlie, cheerfully.

Max pointed out that since Charlie would only get a pound for his tooth (and only fifty pence if the tooth fairy followed their mum's instructions) this proved once again that all this tooth fairy nonsense was a complete waste of time.

'Forget the tooth fairy!' Max advised Charlie.

'No!' said Charlie. 'I've got an idea for a very good plan.'

That night Charlie did not leave
his tooth under his pillow. He left a
carefully written set of instructions.

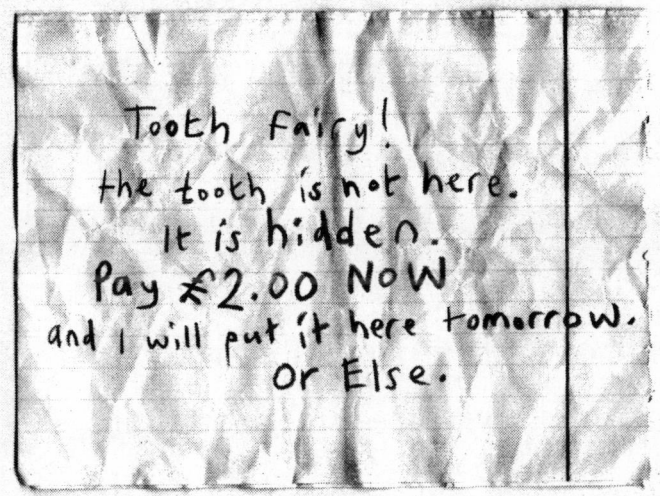

Tooth Fairy!
the tooth is not here.
It is hidden.
Pay £2.00 NOW
and I will put it here tomorrow.
Or Else.

But it seemed that the tooth fairy was
tough, or perhaps she didn't like being
bossed about. Charlie's note was still
there in the morning, but now there was
a message on the back.

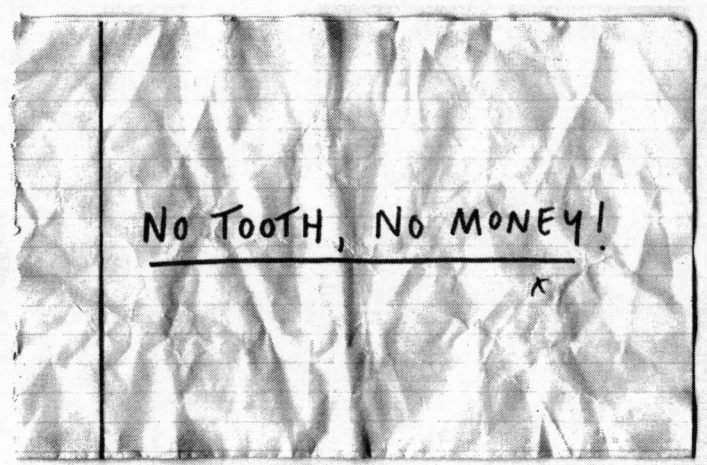

The Third Tooth

'No tooth, no money!' said Charlie, furiously. 'What kind of a fairy is that? What'll I do now?'

'Keep your teeth,' said Max. 'Like I told you before.'

'What were you thinking of?' asked his mother. 'Two pounds for a tooth! Not in this house!'

'It's two pounds for a tooth in Henry's

house,' said Charlie, sulkily. 'And anyway, she could have left me one pound at least! She could have left me something!'

'You didn't leave her anything,' pointed out his mother. 'And you didn't tidy either! Anyway, never mind, you can always put your tooth under your pillow and try again. You'll just have to wait till tomorrow.'

'But I don't want to wait till tomorrow,' protested Charlie.

'Well, if you really don't want to wait till tomorrow,' said his mother, 'you could pretend I am a tooth fairy! I will give you fifty pence to do what you like with for that tooth, and a nice crunchy apple besides.'

'Fifty pence?' asked Charlie, looking at the tooth in his hand. 'Is that all?'

'Yes,' said his mother. 'And a nice crunchy apple, sliced up because you haven't any bottom teeth. And a piece of flapjack just out of the oven if you wait five minutes for it to cool a bit.'

'I bet you give Max a piece of flapjack too,' said Charlie bitterly.

'I probably will,' agreed his mother. 'Since he has just taken the rubbish out, and vacuumed the hall and brushed down the stairs.'

Charlie sighed, and looked at the flapjack.

'What about Henry?' he asked. 'We always share.'

'Oh, all right,' said his mother. 'Here's my final offer. Fifty pence to do what you like with. One crunchy apple sliced up because you haven't any bottom teeth. Two pieces of flapjack, one for Henry.'

'I'll take the money and the flapjack,' said Charlie, at last. 'Forget the apple.'

'The apple was part of the deal,' said the pretend tooth fairy sternly.

Charlie and Henry had a feast at Henry's house. First the apple to get rid of it. Then the flapjack. Then the long red liquorice bootlaces that they had bought with Charlie's fifty pence, and which they made last all afternoon by sucking them like spaghetti in and out of the gaps in their teeth until Henry's mother ordered them to chew them up before she went mad.

And then everything was eaten, and Charlie said, 'What'll we do now?'

'How are your other wobbly teeth?' asked Henry.

Charlie tested them. They were both much wobblier than they had been earlier in the day, particularly one that had got itself stuck in a bite of flapjack.

'You've got quite a bit of movement there,' said Henry, looking at it with interest. 'Keep pushing. I've got a good idea about that tooth.'

'So have I,' said Charlie, 'I'm going to put it under *your* pillow!'

'Under my pillow?'

'Yes, and then I'll get two pounds instead of one.'

'Would that work?' wondered Henry, and he ran downstairs with Charlie after him, and asked his mother, 'Mum, would it work if Charlie put his tooth under my pillow instead of his own?'

'I expect so,' said Henry's mother. 'But why on earth would he want to do that?'

'So as to get two pounds instead of one,' explained Charlie.

'Good grief!' said Henry's mother, looking very startled indeed. 'Are you telling me the tooth fairy gets away with paying just one pound at your house, Charlie?'

Charlie nodded.

'It can't be the same fairy,' said Henry's mother, and then she added, rather hopefully, 'Of course, there is no telling which fairy will come here next time. It might easily never be the two pound one again ...'

'It might be the ten pound note one,' said Henry, glaring at his mother through half closed eyes. 'Have you thought of that?'

'No, no, no,' said his mother, hastily. 'There's no such thing as a ten pound note fairy! Don't be silly, Henry! And don't forget to warn Charlie that the tooth fairy who visits this house only comes for absolutely sparkling clean and tidy bedrooms. So you might want to think again about leaving your next tooth here, Charlie!'

'Oh no,' said Charlie, cheerfully. 'I'm dead quick at tidying up.'

'She checks under the bed,' warned Henry's mother. 'And inside the wardrobe for things in heaps at the bottom. And all the toys have to be sorted into the right boxes and stacked very neatly. And that's before you even start on the vacuuming ...'

'Vacuuming?'

'And dusting ...'

'Dusting?'

'Pairing up socks ...'

'What?'

'Bringing down shoes, and recycling and rubbish! Organizing the bookcase! And (of course) cleaning out that dreadful smelly hamster!'

'He doesn't smell at all!' said Henry, indignantly. 'Only of hamster! Who could mind the lovely smell of hamster? Come on, Charlie! Let's go and do things at your house! Your tooth isn't even out yet!'

'I know, but I think you should tidy up your room ready for when it is.'

'I should tidy it?' asked Henry. 'It's your tooth!'

'It's your mess!'

'It's not just mine!' said Henry. 'It's at least half yours! The den was your idea, and all those tins of mud you stuffed under my bed yesterday.'

'They are not tins of mud,' said Charlie. 'They are Science. They are

a fossil-making machine. That's how fossils are *made,* with mud! If you don't believe me, ask Max. Anyway, if I help you tidy, will you let my tooth go under your pillow?'

'Oh, all right,' agreed Henry.

'It's definitely loosening,' said Charlie, waggling it with a finger as hard as he could bear. 'Do you know any more good ways of getting teeth out quickly?'

'I might be able to remember one,' said Henry cautiously. 'If you let me lie down and think. If you like, *I'll* go to your house and lie down and think in *your* bedroom, while *you* begin tidying in mine.'

'Do you think I'm bonkers?' demanded Charlie. 'We'll *both* lie down and think, and then we'll *both* tidy!'

They started the thinking straight

away, lying side by side amongst the fossil-making machine on Henry's carpet.

Henry finished his thinking first. It was easier for him to think of ways of getting rid of teeth quickly because it was not his tooth that was going to be got rid of. Whenever Charlie had a good tooth-pulling idea it always ended with the worrying question, 'But wouldn't that hurt?' Henry did not have any problems like that, which was how he thought of *The Spectacular Flying Arrow Extraction System,* the same as Robin Hood probably used.

At first Henry kept his idea a secret because if it worked (and he was sure it would) he would have to tidy his bedroom. But it was a hard secret to keep with Charlie beside him muttering, 'What about ... Oh yes! Only wouldn't that hurt?' and jiggling his tooth as he thought, so that it got looser and looser all the time.

It would be a shame, thought Henry, if Charlie's tooth fell out by itself, before he had time to try out his idea. And so he said to Charlie, 'There *is* one very good way ...'

At first Charlie said, 'No.'

'But you want your tooth out!'

'Not like that. It would definitely hurt! I know it would.'

'How can you know till you've tried it?' asked Henry.

'I can guess!'

'Charlie,' said Henry, in a very quiet kind voice, like a dentist. 'I promise you won't feel a thing. (Hardly.) It's the way everyone did it in the olden days, before they had upstairs windows and remote control cars.'

'I'll just wobble it,' said Charlie, and for the next two days that was what he did.

And for the next two days, Henry said, 'Oh, come on, let me do it! There's nothing on telly! I'm so bored!'

'Don't let Henry pull your teeth out just because there's nothing on telly!' Max told Charlie.

'I won't,' said Charlie.

So the third wobbly tooth stayed where it was.

It was loose. It was so loose Charlie could stick it out between his two closed lips, like a fang.

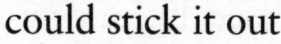

But it didn't come out.

And there was nothing on telly.

And Charlie was bored too.

So at last he said, 'OK, Henry. Fetch the dental floss!'

With *The Spectacular Flying Arrow Extraction System*, the end of the thread that was not fastened to Charlie's tooth was tied to an arrow from Charlie's bow and arrow set.

Then Charlie and Henry went into the

garden and Henry said, 'Now give me the bow.'

'No,' said Charlie. 'Not this time! I gave you the remote control handset and look what happened!'

Charlie fitted the arrow to the bowstring himself.

And then he pulled back the string as far as it would go.

And he stood like that for quite a long time, until Henry suddenly shouted, 'Fire!' and Charlie, who was not expecting him to do this, jumped in surprise.

The arrow flew into the air, and Charlie's tooth went with it.

FIRE!

Higher and higher they soared, in a wonderful curve with nothing but blue sky behind. And they landed perfectly safely at the end of the garden.

And after that the only thing left to do was tidy Henry's bedroom. Which took ages.

The Fourth Tooth

The next day Charlie called for Henry at half past five in the morning.

'Goodness, Charlie,' groaned Henry's mum, blinking and yawning on the doorstep. 'Did you have to ring the bell *and* hammer quite so hard? I'm sure ...'

But Charlie had already hurried past her into the house, raced up the stairs to

Henry's bedroom, shoved his sleeping friend out of the way, and snatched aside his pillow.

'Go awayyyyy!' groaned Henry, as his head hit the mattress. 'Gerroff my bed! Give me back my pillow!'

'Got it!' rejoiced Charlie, grabbing an envelope from beside Henry's ear.

'Good. Go home then,' said Henry.

Charlie did not go home. He bounced down on to the

 bed, ripped open the envelope, and tipped into his hand two

lovely round pound coins.

Then Charlie got very noisy indeed, jumping round the bedroom, shouting, 'Ha! Brilliant! Amazing!' and singing, 'I tricked the tooth fairy! I tricked the tooth fairy!' and shaking Henry and demanding that he wake up properly, and look.

Henry groaned, rubbed his eyes, looked and remarked, 'You ought to give one of them to me!'

'I'm not!' said Charlie.

'That's mean then! It was my idea that got the tooth out! And my pillow that you put it under. In my bedroom that I had to help tidy. It was MY tooth fairy!'

'It was MY tooth!' said Charlie.

'Show-off!'

'Grabber!'

'Greedy pig!'

'Like your pyjamas!' jeered Charlie, which was particularly unkind because they were the Thomas the Tank Engine ones that Henry vowed he never wore.

So then Henry got on top of Charlie with his beanbag and squashed him flat.

Charlie went all silent and limp to frighten him.

'You've not fainted or something, have you?'

asked Henry, lifting off the beanbag, and Charlie lunged out, got him round the knees, rolled him up in his quilt and pushed him under his bed.

Henry sat up under his bed, burst through the wooden slats that made the base, and heaved the mattress at his friend.

The bookcase fell over and so did the hamster cage. The fossil-making machine was wrecked. Henry's mother came in and said in a dreadful voice, 'STOP!'

Charlie and Henry tidied Henry's bedroom in absolute silence while Henry's mother stood in the doorway and glared. When it was done she said, 'Henry, you are grounded.

Charlie, go home.'

Charlie had been sent home in disgrace from Henry's house many times before, probably almost as many as Henry had been sent home from Charlie's house. So he went away quite cheerfully. He was feeling very pleased with himself. He had successfully tricked the tooth fairy with his third wobbly tooth. He had seen Henry wearing Thomas the Tank Engine pyjamas with his own eyes. And he had two pounds to do what he liked with.

That afternoon Charlie spent the whole two pounds on a giant bag of butterscotch popcorn that he took out into the street to show Henry, who was staring gloomily through his bedroom

window, still grounded.

Charlie mimed gobbling the popcorn all up.

Henry mimed jumping out of the window and killing him.

Charlie mimed that he would save the last crumb for Henry.

Henry turned down his mouth and shrugged his shoulders to show that he couldn't care less.

Then Charlie swaggered on down the street, but when he turned back to wave before going into his own house he caught sight of Henry's face.

Henry was not miming. He just looked sad.

So Charlie went inside feeling awful and the first thing he did was go and hunt for Max. And not long afterwards he came out of his house again, and ran back down the street to Henry's front door.

Charlie knocked on Henry's door with his best respectful knocking, and when Henry's mother opened it he said in his politest voice, 'Please, I am very sorry I woke you up so early in the morning and wrecked Henry's bedroom and fought him (he started it, though) and please may I go up and be grounded with him too? Because that is only fair, Max said. And I really am sorry, not

just saying it. I promise. If you don't believe me, ask Max.'

'All right, Charlie,' said Henry's mother, at last.

It was brilliant being grounded with Henry. They turned Henry's bedroom into a cinema by drawing the curtains and watched telly all afternoon with the bag of popcorn between them.

At first they talked about what they would buy when Charlie's fourth wobbly tooth fell out, and how important it was to keep the bedroom tidy so as to be able to trick the tooth fairy again. And they talked about popcorn, and how much they liked the hard crunchy bits that were solid butterscotch, and how Charlie always sucked them, and how Henry always munched them up quick.

But soon they stopped talking. They were sleepy from being up so early. They chomped and watched telly and chomped and dreamed and forgot about teeth. Popcorn got spilled and was

eaten off the floor. Charlie was half asleep when Henry suddenly remembered an idea he had had while he was busy being grounded and said, 'So what about making a tooth fairy trap?'

Charlie was so suprised that a handful of popcorn went down the wrong way and he choked and coughed it all over the floor. And in the fuss of picking it up again the whole bag was knocked over. From downstairs Henry's mum, who seemed to have developed the power to see through ceilings, called warningly, 'Henry! Charlie!'

'Pick it up,' whispered Henry urgently, 'before she comes up and goes mad again. She's been awful all day.'

They scrabbled about on their hands and knees in the dim cinema light, collecting popcorn and tidying it into their mouths as they found it.

'Isn't it strange,' remarked Henry, crunching a particularly hard piece of butterscotch, 'how the top bit of the bag tastes fantastic, and the middle bit is OK but boring, and the last bit is just nasty but you can't seem to stop ... CHARLIE! Your tooth!'

'What?'

'Put the light on! Put the light on!' squeaked Henry, and raced and put it on himself.

But all at once Charlie did not need light to know what had happened.

It had gone. His fourth and last wobbly tooth. Vanished, all by itself, with no help from anyone.

'*Where* has it gone?' moaned Henry, because the switching on of the light had revealed something even more shocking. Amongst the spilled and scattered popcorn all over the floor there were pieces that were stained with …

'Blood!' howled Henry. 'No wonder it didn't taste right!' 'Oh, what does it matter what it tasted like?' wailed

Charlie. 'Help me find my tooth!'

But the tooth could not be found. Charlie and Henry searched and searched. So did Max, when they fetched him to help them. They looked under everything, and on top of everything, and between everything.

They picked up every fragment of popcorn, and every piece they picked up looked like a tooth.

They carried on searching until there was no doubt left at all.

And then Max made the awful announcement.

'One of you,' said Max, 'must have eaten it.'

'*Eaten my tooth*?' asked Charlie.

'By mistake,' said Max.

'But you'd know!' said Charlie. 'It would be hard! It would crunch!'

Henry groaned. He knew who had eaten

Charlie's tooth. He had guessed it ages ago. He could even feel it, like a tooth-shaped nightmare in the middle of his stomach.

In the kitchen, the mothers were drinking coffee and complaining about the amount of sweets Charlie and Henry ate (which they thought were far too many) and the school holidays (which they thought were far too long) when the boys burst in.

'What does the tooth fairy do,' demanded Charlie, 'if the tooth gets eaten?'

'What?' exclaimed the mothers. 'Who's eaten a tooth?'

'Henry has!'

'I didn't even know he had wobbly

64

ones,' said Henry's mother, very surprised.

'He doesn't. It was mine,' said Charlie, showing them his latest gory gap.

'Henry ate your tooth?' asked Charlie's mother.

'He crunched it up. He thought it was popcorn ... Oh, stop laughing! It isn't funny! What I need to know is, does the tooth fairy *have to have the actual tooth*?'

'Yes!' said both mothers instantly.

Teeth

Charlie said it wasn't fair.

'Just because she's called a fairy doesn't mean she's fair,' said his mother.

'Besides,' said Henry's mother, 'you and Henry have had enough sweets lately to last you for months.'

'There must be something we can do,' said Charlie. 'What about if we put *the whole* of Henry under his pillow?'

The mothers shook their heads. '*Tidily* under his pillow?' asked Charlie, remembering the extreme fussiness of the tooth fairy. 'No,' said the mothers cheerfully. 'Wouldn't work.'

'Why not?'

'Because there wouldn't be a tooth, would there?' explained Henry's mother. 'Not an actual tooth that anyone could take away.'

'No tooth, no money!' Charlie's mother reminded him.

'Well,' said Charlie, desperately,

'let's take Henry to hospital to have an operation to get it back again.'

'An operation!' squealed Henry. 'What sort of operation?'

'A getting-my-tooth-back-operation!'

'How?'

'Well, I suppose they'd slice you open or something,' said Charlie sulkily.

'No!' yelled Henry, and the mothers explained that doctors and surgeons were far too busy to slice people open for the sake of a swallowed tooth, no matter who it belonged to.

'I *hate* the tooth fairy!' growled Charlie.

'So do I!' said Henry.

'Come with me,' said Max.

Max and Charlie shared a bedroom, but that did not mean that they did not each have their own private places. Charlie, for instance, had an old brown bear that was practically hollow. Max had ...

Charlie didn't know what Max had. Max was clever. Max's secrets were hidden.

But now Max led Charlie and Henry to a battered grey box in the corner of the bedroom labelled: HOMEWORK SHEETS.

From the homework sheets box Max took a pair of football socks, unwashed and rolled into a ball.

From the middle of the ball of football socks he unwrapped a very small book which he handed to Charlie.

COLLINS ENGLISH DICTIONARY,
it said on the cover.

'So what?' asked Charlie, and Max
laughed.

Charlie and Henry looked at each
other, completely puzzled, because
who could be pleased to be shown a
dictionary, especially a dictionary
that came out of a ball of dirty
socks? Socks from a box labelled

HOMEWORK SHEETS.

'Open it,' said Max.

It was not a book, it was a book made into a box. The pages had been glued together, and a rough rectangular hollow cut in the middle of them, so that when the front cover was lifted a secret space was revealed.

In that secret space were teeth.

Max shook them and they rattled like strange small stones, cream coloured, faintly gleaming. A weird, eerie collection of chisel-edged front teeth

and back ones like a miniature range of ancient hills.

'Twelve so far,' said Max, and then he wrapped them carefully up again, put them in his pocket and went away.

Charlie and Henry had seen some cool things in their lives.

Their friend Sam had a fake stick-on wound that made anywhere he stuck it look sliced wide open.

At a Halloween party they had been given blood-red jelly with plastic glow in the dark fingernails sprinkled on the top.

In Science they had seen a model of a person whose skin lifted off in sections to show his life-size multicoloured bulging insides.

They had thought those things were cool.

But in all their lives they had never seen anything as cool as Max's secret collection of teeth.

They were not models, or plastic, or fake from the joke shop.

They were real.

'I wish I'd kept my teeth!' said Charlie sadly.

'Yes, think what you could do,' agreed Henry, 'if you had a whole lot like that?'

'You could make a fantastic cannibal necklace.'

'You could make a horror mask with plasticine lips and real teeth.'

'Imagine freezing them. Trick ice cubes for parties!'

'Or you could just keep them for ever,' said Henry. 'In a hollowed out book, like Max's. That book was amazing!'

'Let's make one each,' said Charlie.

'Yes,' said Henry, eagerly. 'And fill them with teeth! Our teeth! Who'll have the next wobbly one?'

'If you do,' said Charlie, 'I can help you get it out! I've nearly finished inventing *The Washing Line Zip Wire Easy Out Experience*!'

'If you do,' said Henry, 'there's *The Tasty Toffee Tooth Tugger* that we haven't tried yet!'

'But what about the tooth fairy?' asked Charlie and Henry's mothers when they heard the latest news.

'If we get rid of the tooth fairy we'll never have to tidy our bedrooms again!' said Henry.

'The tooth fairy,' said Charlie, 'is for kids!'

'What kind of person,' asked Henry scornfully, 'sells their own teeth?'

'And who wants fairies crawling round their beds when they're asleep?' added Charlie.

'Not me!' said Henry.

'The tooth fairy,' said Charlie, 'is a waste of teeth. And if you don't believe us, ask Max!'

Charlie and the Big Birthday Bash

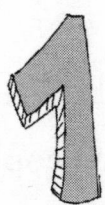

Tuesday. Four days before the Big Bash.
The Amazing Idea day

Charlie's house was in a very nice street. There was never much traffic because it didn't go anywhere. It

was the sort of street where you could play outside. The pavements were wide enough for scooters and

roller skates. Cats could walk about and not get run over. In warm weather front doors stood open and dogs slept in gardens.

Charlie knew who lived in every house. Some of the people were friends, like Henry, his best friend, and Lulu, the girl with a million pets. Some were just normal. Some were his enemies. That made the street an interesting place, Charlie thought.

In Charlie's house, there lived his cat, Suzy, his mum and dad, and his big brother, Max.

Suzy was an OK sort of cat.

Charlie's parents were an OK sort of parents.

But Max was a very good brother

indeed. Max hardly ever got mad when Charlie borrowed his stuff.

And he got wonderful marks when he did Charlie's homework.

And he spent hours trying to teach Charlie how to do good things, like whistling with his fingers, or climbing through the trapdoor into the attic.

'And he's always getting you out of trouble,' said Charlie's friend Henry, enviously. Henry did not have any brothers, big or little. If he was in trouble, he either had to stay in it or get out of it by himself.

Henry said Charlie was lucky to have Max.

'Well, Max is lucky to have me,' said Charlie.

Charlie did things for Max too. Not useful things like homework, or clever things like whistling, or brave things like when Max went with Charlie to explain to the Yellow Car Man, who lived next door to Henry, why two football boots had accidentally been thrown through the windscreen of his lovely yellow sports car.

What Charlie did for Max was Surprises.

Charlie thought surprises were the best things in the world. They were the opposite of boring, which was the worst thing in the world.

The sort of surprises Charlie arranged for Max were:

Surprise Wanted posters made on Henry's computer and stuck up in surprising places, like Max's school bus stop.

Surprise wild animals in his bed.

Surprise messages in his homework diary.

Absolutely wonderful brilliant

surprises, like the time Max left his wellies outside on the doorstep, and Charlie filled them up with water and put them in the freezer for the night.

And then back out on the doorstep in the morning.

Max couldn't believe it when he found them. He showed them to everyone. He phoned up his friends. He couldn't stop listening to the weather forecast.

He was very, very surprised.

Now Charlie was planning Max's biggest surprise of all.

'It's his birthday at the weekend,' he told Henry, as they walked home from school together, 'and guess what sort of a birthday party he's having?'

'What?' asked Henry eagerly, because he and Charlie loved parties and went to as many as possible.

'*No* birthday party,' said Charlie.

'No birthday party?' repeated Henry. '*No birthday party?*'

'Yes.'

'You mean no *actual* birthday *actual* party? Do you *actually* mean that?'

'Yes I do,' said Charlie.

'What did Max do to make your mum say no birthday party?' Henry asked, in a very shocked voice. Before his own last birthday, Henry had done something so awful that the party had been very nearly, extremely nearly, practically certainly, cancelled.

If Max wasn't having a birthday party, he must have done something even worse.

What was worse, Henry wondered, than trapping the all-night babysitter in the cupboard under the stairs and then going to bed and falling instantly asleep for ten hours?

'Nothing,' said Charlie.

'Nothing?' asked Henry.

'Mum didn't say no birthday party,'

said Charlie. '*Max* said no birthday party! He says he doesn't like parties.'

'He's mad,' said Henry. 'Parties are the only time you ever get party food!'

'Max doesn't like party food,' said Charlie.

'What?' asked Henry. 'Jelly and sausage rolls? Pink biscuits and crisps and bits of pizza gone cold! All that lovely stuff, Max doesn't like?'

'No, and he hates birthday cake too because he doesn't like icing. And he says party games are boring. But dancing is his worst thing

of all. Once he went to a party that was *all* dancing and somebody made him do the conga. So Max climbed out of a window and caught a bus and came home. Max says dancing is scary!'

'But Max is brave!' protested Henry. 'Look how brave he was with the Yellow Car Man!'

'I know,' agreed Charlie. 'Max is very brave! It's not just the Yellow Car Man he's brave with either. He rescued me from Old Mashed Potatoes *again* last night.'

Old Mashed Potatoes was Miss Ash. Charlie and Henry called her Old Mashed Potatoes for short. The Yellow Car Man was one of the enemies who

lived on Charlie's street. Old Mashed
Potatoes was the other. She lived next
door to Charlie's family and she was
a teacher at Max's school. She taught
maths.

'Fancy living next door to a maths
teacher!' complained Charlie. 'You
might as well live next door to a
cannibal.'

Max didn't mind Miss Ash. He earned
extra pocket money mowing her lawn.

'She likes him,' said Charlie. 'She likes
Max and Mum and Dad and Suzy, but
she doesn't like me.'

This was true. Miss Ash never had
been friends with Charlie. This was
because once when he was three years
old, he had tunnelled under the fence

between the gardens and picked all her daffodils. He had then dragged them back through the hole he had made, all squashed and muddy, and given them to his mum for a present.

'How sweet,' Miss Ash had said over the garden fence. 'As if I minded!'

But she did mind. She had blocked up Charlie's hole with rocks. And ever since then she had not liked Charlie. She didn't like him climbing on the fence. She didn't like him drawing pictures on the pavement with chalk. She told his mum when he sang the Old Mashed Potato song.

'So what did you do to Old Mashed Potatoes *this* time?' asked Henry.

'Nothing!' said Charlie. 'It was nothing to do with her! All I was doing was seeing how far the new hose pipe would reach. And it reached her garden and she went mad: as if it was my fault my dad buys such scary hose pipes that they come alive in your hands.'

'What do you mean? Come alive in your hands?'

'That's what it did when I turned it on full power. It was like a giant snake gone crazy! Everything got soaking wet. I couldn't help it.'

'Did it hit Old Mashed Potatoes, then?'

'No. Well, hardly. More her washing. But she made such a fuss! She didn't calm down until Max went round and mowed her lawn for free.'

'Max is brilliant,' said Henry. 'He should have a party! He deserves a party, even if he doesn't want one.'

'He's going to have one,' said Charlie, smirking. 'That's my amazing idea! *I'm going to arrange for Max to have a great big surprise birthday –*'

'Party!' finished Henry, bouncing with excitement.

'*Bash*,' corrected Charlie, 'because Max doesn't like parties.

Wednesday. Three days before the Big Bash.
Everything You Need for a Bash

'*B*ash!' sang Henry, because he liked the sound of the word, '*Bash, oh bash! Oh bash! Bash! Bash!*'

'Shut up!' said Charlie, looking nervously up and down the street. 'It's a secret! This bash is supposed to be a surprise!'

'I'll not tell,' sang Henry. 'Never-ever-ever-ever! Oh bash!'

Charlie took off his sweatshirt and tied it by the sleeves over Henry's face. After Henry was gagged and blindfolded, Charlie guided his friend into a bush. Sometimes you had to do things like that to Henry.

Henry got better in the bush. He came out quite calm and normal.

'When my mum organized my party,' he said, 'she made lists. Lists of who'd come. Lists of games. Lists of food. So it was all organized.'

'Your party wasn't organized!' said Charlie, very surprised. 'Your mum even lost the cake! It was good, but it wasn't organized.'

'It was meant to be, though,' said Henry.

'Oh.'

'Didn't you notice?' asked Henry in a rather hurt voice.

'Well, of course I did,' agreed Charlie, kindly. 'And I suppose it did get a bit calmer after the ambulance had gone. Until the bath overflowed … Do you think we could have Max's party at your house, Henry? Ours is no good because Max would see us getting ready and it would spoil the surprise.'

'Ours is no good either,' said Henry. 'Because after that last (very organized, thank you) party, my mum said never ever ever again. Never. Not in a million years. In fact, she said the next party she gives will be in the street ... with our front door locked ...'

'Henry!' shouted Charlie. 'That's perfect!'

'What's perfect?'

'A party in the street!'

Even as Charlie spoke, he saw a picture in his mind of a party in the street. Crowds and games and music. Tables piled with food. Balloons and streamers. A great big banner ...

'You couldn't really have a party in

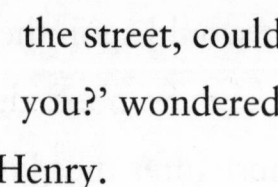

the street, could you?' wondered Henry.

'Of course you could!' said Charlie, and rushed home to make the banner.

Henry stomped into his own house and asked his mum, 'Did you mean it when you said about a party in the street? A birthday party, I mean. Would it be allowed?'

Henry's mother groaned.

'Not a birthday party for *me*,' said Henry, hastily. 'For someone else.'

'Charlie?' asked his mum, interestedly. 'No, Charlie's had his birthday, hasn't he? Max?'

'Stop guessing! It's a secret. But is it

allowed?'

'It's a very good idea,' said Henry's
mother.

Charlie made a banner like a row of
coloured flags.

SURPRISE!

He wrote it on the flags in enormous
bright letters and took it round to show
Henry. A terrible noise from
Henry's house told him
that once again,
Henry had found
his recorder.

'Parties need
music,' Henry
said.

'Do they?'
asked

Charlie doubtfully. 'How did you get that recorder from down the back of the radiator?'

'How did you know it was down the back of the radiator?' asked Henry.

'Just a guess.'

'Well, lucky for you that I did. It's just what we need. Think! Pass the parcel, musical bumps …'

'Those are just the sort of baby party games that Max hates.'

'Karaoke …'

'Karaoke on your recorder?' asked Charlie.

'Absolutely,' said Henry proudly, and began to play a selection of tunes from the beginning pages of *Recorder Book One*.

After his sixth time through 'Twinkle, Twinkle, Little Star', Charlie wrestled his friend to the floor.

Henry's mother heard the bumps and ordered them outside.

'We were just going,' said Charlie, smiling up at her from Henry's chest, and Henry added, 'No one needs to yell!'

The fascinating yellow sports car was parked outside, repaired after its adventure with the football boots.

Its shining sides were covered in a smooth layer of summer dust. When Charlie touched it, his finger left a shiny yellow spot.

They continued planning the party.

'Food,' said Charlie.

'Food,' agreed Henry, shaking spit from his recorder. 'A lot.'

'Yes, a lot,' nodded Charlie. 'Hmm.' And he drew a long wriggly snake with a spotted back and a forked tongue on the sports car's bonnet while he thought.

'I wouldn't do that if I were you,' said Henry, a bit nervously.

Charlie ignored him and wrote MAX
in loopy letters in the lovely smooth
dust.

'We'll have all his
favourite things,'
he told Henry.

'What
are his
favourites?'
asked Henry,
taking a few steps
away from Charlie.

Charlie thought,
trying to remember the
lists of foods that he and Max recited to
each other after days out, when they sat
starving in the back of the car, longing
to be home.

'Apple pie,' he remembered. 'Marmite on toast … you can never cook Max too much marmite on toast … bananas …'

'That's not enough for a party, though,' said Henry.

'I know … let me think … apple pie, marmite toast, bananas …'

'*Charlie!*' exclaimed Henry, suddenly.

'What?'

'He'll kill you!' said Henry, pointing.

There were more pictures in the lovely dust now, some bananas, a lot of toast, and a large apple pie.

'I'm going in,' said Henry.

'It'll wipe off,' said

Charlie. 'Anyway, I've stopped now.'

All the same, he could not resist adding a few wisps of curly steam rising from the apple pie. It was the best pie he'd ever drawn. It looked good enough to eat.

'Goodbye,' said Henry.

Charlie did not even notice he had gone.

'Apple pie,' he murmured. 'Marmite toast, bananas and ... and ... and ...'

What was it, Max's favourite food? Charlie could almost see it. He could almost hear Max's voice, saying, 'Best of all, I should like ...' Charlie could almost smell it ... He *could* smell it ...

'CURRY!' wrote Charlie triumphantly.

'OI!' bellowed a very cross voice.

The owner of the yellow sports car had opened his front door.

Out poured the smell of the curry he was cooking.

Out roared the owner of the car.

'I MIGHT HAVE KNOWN! I MIGHT HAVE KNOWN!' he kept shouting, although what he might have known he did not say.

Still, Charlie could tell that he did not like the drawings on his car, not even when Charlie explained that he had done them without thinking, while planning Max's party.

The Yellow Car Man glared and said, 'I might have known!' even at the apple pie. And then he fetched a bucket of water and very carefully, while still muttering, washed his car clean. He had a special squeaky car sponge that made bubbles as soft and thick as whipped cream. Charlie would have liked a go with that sponge, and several times he offered very politely to help, but the Yellow Car Man would not share. He did not even like it when Charlie collected up the bubbles that ran away in the gutter. Charlie made them into a midsummer snowman on the pavement outside Henry's gate. The Yellow Car

Man glared at it before he marched back into his house. Then there was a smell of curry as his door opened again, and then he was gone.

'I told you so,' said Henry, reappearing.

Charlie converted the midsummer snowman into midsummer snowballs.

And very soon afterwards Henry rolled Charlie in a midsummer snowdrift.

And in the middle of this the smell of curry became very strong again as the Yellow Car Man stood on his doorstep

to make sure no soap splodges landed
on his beautiful yellow car.

'Curry,' said Charlie. 'That's
Max's favourite food that I couldn't
remember.'

'Curry,' said Henry. 'Oh.'

And then he said, 'I know what. We'll
share getting the food. I'll do the boring
marmite toast and bananas, because
I'm not a relation – just someone who
lives down the street – and you do the
much more exciting curry and apple pie,
because Max is your brother and that
makes you *really important*! OK?'

'OK,' said Charlie. 'Really important!
Yes! OK!'

3

Thursday. Two days before the Big Bash.
Invitation Day

They made invitations on Henry's computer.

EVERYBODY COME TO THE

BIRTHDAY BASH

ON SATURDAY AFTERNOON AT 3

AT MAX AND CHARLIE'S STREET

DON'T
TELL
MAX

BECAUSE IT'S A
SURPRISE!

They printed off dozens and then Charlie went home and after he was gone Henry looked at the invitations again.

It doesn't say enough, he thought. And it's not just Max and Charlie's street either.

So all by himself he made another set.

EVERYBODY COME TO THE

BIRTHDAY BASH

ON SATURDAY AFTERNOON AT 3

AT MAX AND CHARLIE'S STREET

DON'T
TELL
MAX

BECAUSE IT'S A
SURPRISE!

KARAOKE WITH HENRY ON RECORDER!

NO BORING PARTY GAMES

SO BRING SOMETHING

EXCITING

TO DO INSTEAD (HENRY'S IDEA)

INVITATIONS DESIGNED AND PRINTED BY HENRY ON HENRY'S COMPUTER

'You've ruined them!' said Charlie when he saw them. 'They're just one big show off about you! I'm putting them in the bin!'

He grabbed them.

Henry grabbed them back.

This went on for a very long time, while Charlie and Henry scuffled and snatched and chased each other in and out of their houses and up and down the street.

The invitations began to look rather scruffy.

And then they were accidentally dropped.

It was a windy day. Crumpled pieces of paper blew all down the street. Into gardens.

Under cars. Down into drains and up into trees. It took ages to pick them up.

So that was the end of the invitations.

'Now I suppose I'll have to make another set,' said Henry, crossly. 'Bother!'

'You needn't bother,' said Charlie. '*I'll* sort out the invitations.'

Secretly he was a bit pleased that

the invitations were lost. Once the invitations were sent, the party would have to happen. That was good, except for one thing.

Food.

Charlie wished that he was doing the bananas and toast and marmite, and Henry was doing the curry and the apple pie.

The very scary curry and the terrifying apple pie.

The nightmare curry and the sleep-haunting apple pie.

But he didn't intend to admit that to Henry, so instead he said, 'There's things we need to sort out first before we do more invitations.'

'Like what?'

'Like decorations.'

'Easy,' said Henry. 'We've millions in a box in the cupboard under the stairs. Left over from Christmas. There's even balloons.'

'And what people will do.'

'I sorted that in the invitations,' said Henry grumpily. 'I said bring exciting things. If twenty people come, that's twenty exciting things to do. If forty people come, that's forty exciting things! If sixty –'

'Sixty!' exploded Charlie. 'If sixty people come, what will sixty people eat? You haven't sorted that!'

'I nearly have, though,' said Henry smugly. 'We've a new jar of marmite, and I've got a loads of bananas under my bed. I'll get even more when I visit my gran. So all we really need is for you to get the curry ready ...'

Charlie groaned.

'And the apple pie.'

Friday. One day before the Big Bash.
Charlie's Cooking Day

Charlie got up very early on Friday morning.

'Mum,' he said. 'Can I learn to cook?'

'Certainly,' she agreed. 'Everyone should learn to cook. What would you like to make?'

'Curry,' Charlie told her.

Charlie's mum said he should start with something much easier, like Ready

Brek or scrambled eggs. She showed him how.

Charlie made Ready Brek with secret added curry powder. It was awful. He made scrambled eggs with secret added curry and they were the worst eggs in the world.

'Can't I leave you alone for five seconds?' demanded his mother when she saw what he had done, and then she left him alone for much more than five seconds while she went and answered the phone.

Charlie thought hard about what curry looked like. Orangey, lumpy, vegetabley stuff.

Then very quickly he mixed baked beans and soup and curry powder.

He added lumps of cheese to make
it bumpier, tomato sauce to make it
redder, yellow paint from his paint box
to make it yellower and biscuit crumbs
to make it stiffer. He thought it looked a
bit like curry.

Then Charlie's mum came back into
the kitchen and went unsurprisingly
bonkers. She
ordered Charlie
to throw his
curry away,
and chased
him out of
kitchen.

Charlie
put his curry
into a secret

bucket which he hid in his cupboard upstairs.

After school he showed it to Henry.

Henry suggested more sauce, some cold pasta, peanuts and sweetcorn, and he fetched these things from his own house and added them before Charlie could stop him.

'One good thing,' said Henry, stirring it with a stolen spoon. 'There's loads!'

There was loads, but it was pinkish so they added mustard and coffee. Then it was the right colour but smelled odd so they put in lemon juice.

'Shouldn't it be in the fridge?' asked Henry. 'So it doesn't get germs?'

In case of germs Charlie poured in cough medicine.

'I wonder what it tastes like,' said Henry, but added almost at once, 'I don't eat curry. I have thirty-one bananas from visiting both grans and plenty of marmite. So now you only have to arrange the apple pie.'

Charlie asked his mother, 'How do you make apple pie?'

'I don't think I can cope with any more cooking lessons at the moment, Charlie,' said his mother.

'How do you make apple pie?' Charlie asked his father.

Charlie's father was probably the worst cook in the world (after Charlie), so he had to think hard.

'Apple pie?' he asked. 'Max's favourite! Good idea. Well, obviously it's apple underneath, isn't it, with ... um ... pie on top. Mashed apple obviously, and flat ... er ... flat pie. With a rolling pin,' said Charlie's father triumphantly. 'Perfectly simple!'

Charlie thought he would do the underneath first, and so he took three apples, the potato masher, a large pie dish and a rolling pin, and went down to the end of the garden.

At first the apples would not mash. Certainly not with the potato masher. It was like trying to mash stones, or shoes, or something not mashable. Charlie gave up and attacked the apples with the rolling pin. He whacked them until they smashed. He pounded them until they flew out of the dish. He got apple in his hair and all down his front. Sometimes he pounded his fingers instead of the apples. Sometimes apple juice squirted into his eyes.

'Curse these apples!' growled Charlie, but he did not give up. He sucked his sore fingers and rubbed his stinging

eyes and attacked the apples again with the rolling pin in one hand and the potato masher in the other.

All the apples shot out of the bowl and escaped on to the grass.

'Curse and curse and curse these apples!' howled Charlie.

'What are you doing?' asked a very surprised voice, and there was Old Mashed Potatoes staring over the fence.

'You tell me off for staring over the fence,' said Charlie, glaring at her.

'I know,' she admitted. 'I just heard … I couldn't help wondering … what *are* you doing to those apples, Charlie?'

'Tell off … tell off … tell off …' said Charlie. 'Just because I picked those flowers when I was little!'

'No, no!' said Old Mashed Potatoes. 'You mustn't think that!'

'That hose pipe wasn't meant to go in your garden. It went where it liked. I couldn't stop it!'

'Yes, Max explained. I'm very sorry …'

'I sing,' said Charlie, 'and you tell my mum! If you sang, I wouldn't tell your mum!'

'Charlie, I –'

'And now you're staring at me! I don't suppose you'd like it if I stared at you while you made apple pie!'

'Apple pie!' exclaimed Old Mashed Potatoes. 'Is that what it is?'

'Of course,' said Charlie.

'It's not how I make apple pie,' said Old Mashed Potatoes.

Charlie's apples were now smashed to brownish-orange juicy pieces. Pips and skin and grass were mixed in with the apple. Charlie scooped them out with his fingers. He wiped his fingers on his T-shirt and mopped his face with his sleeve.

'Do you like cooking?' asked Old Mashed Potatoes.

'No,' said Charlie. 'I hate it.'

Then Charlie stood up and kicked the apple pie dish as hard as he could. Mashed-up apple sprayed over the garden.

'Now I've got to start again,' said Charlie, and bent his head.

Old Mashed Potatoes kindly did not look.

But her voice said, 'I quite like cooking. Especially apple pie. What kind of apple pie were you going to make?'

Charlie sniffed.

'A hot one or a cold one?' asked Old Mashed Potatoes. 'A large one or a small one? A square one or a round one?'

'A birthday one,' said Charlie, wiping his nose on his jeans. 'Apple pie is Max's favourite, and tomorrow is his birthday.'

'A birthday cake apple pie! What a wonderful idea!' said Old Mashed Potatoes.

Then Old Mashed Potatoes and Charlie made friends.

The last thing that happened on Friday evening was that Charlie took his bucket of curry to Henry's house to store in Henry's shed.

On the way he met the Yellow Car Man.

The Yellow Car Man looked in his bucket. He looked, and he stared, and he asked, 'What's that?'

'Curry,' said Charlie.

'It's not,' said the Yellow Car Man.

'It is,' said Charlie.

'Curry like you told me about? Curry like you said was your brother Max's favourite food? Curry like you wrote on my car?'

'Yes,' said Charlie.

'It's not,' said the Yellow Car Man.

5
Saturday morning.
Not What you Need for a Bash

Max was still asleep when Charlie woke up on Saturday morning. Charlie, who slept in the bottom bunk, kicked the underside of Max's top bunk until he woke up.

'Max! Max!' he called. 'You'll miss your school bus!'

Max fell out of bed, charged to the bathroom, stuck his head under

the shower and then came back into
the bedroom dripping and said, 'It's
Saturday!'

'Is it?' asked Charlie, in pretend
surprise. 'Gosh, goodness! How
amazing! Ow! Get off! You're all wet!
Put me down! Happy birthday! I've got
you a present! Do you want it?'

Max said of course he did, stopped
sweeping the floor with Charlie's head,
and unwrapped the pair of enormous

black sunglasses that Charlie had
chosen for him.

'Absolutely just what I needed most in
the world,' he said, putting them on at
once.

At breakfast there were more presents:
a beanie hat from Gran. Malteasers
from Suzy the cat. A skateboard and a
camera from Mum and Dad.

'Fantastic,' said Max, and took
photos of everyone – Charlie in the
sunglasses, Suzy in the hat, Mum and

Dad on the skateboard.

Henry came round while Max was still doing it, and asked, in his most innocent voice, 'What's everyone doing today?'

'Same boring stuff as usual,' said Charlie, exploding inside with secret laughter.

'Nothing much,' said Charlie's mum, who usually spent Saturdays in a tearing rush of shopping and gardening and hoovering and catching up on all the jobs she had not had time to do all week.

'Standing around,' said Charlie's dad, who usually spent Saturdays mending everything that had got broken during the week, mowing the lawn, working

out what had happened to his money
and trying to squeeze in a bit of football
but never managing more than a few
minutes.

'Taking photos,' said Max, and took
photos of Henry playing his recorder,
Lulu with three dogs on leads and two
rabbits loose, Old Mashed Potatoes

whispering with his mother over the
fence, the Yellow Car Man smirking
beside his yellow car, and many other

smiling neighbours who all seemed to know without being told that today was Max's birthday.

After that, Max set off into town to photograph Important Places, such as school, and the best chip shop, and the rubbish bin where Charlie's head had got jammed and the fire brigade had had to cut him out. And when he had gone Charlie's parents looked at each other and said, 'Goodness we must rush!' and Henry went home to try and untangle the vast pile of Christmas decorations he had dragged out from under the stairs, and Charlie went next door and made a giant apple pie with Old Mashed Potatoes, his new friend.

'When do you need it?' asked Old

Mashed Potatoes. 'Now or later?'

'Later, for a surprise,' said Charlie.

They left the pie on the table to cool while Old Mashed Potatoes went shopping for birthday candles, and Charlie rushed down to Henry's.

Henry was admiring a mountain of bananas, stolen from the fruit bowls of all his relations. Also he had borrowed the toaster and carried it to his bedroom, opened the new jar of marmite and defrosted two large loaves from the freezer by wrapping them in his quilt.

'Didn't your mum notice?' asked Charlie, but Henry replied that his mum was not noticing things today.

'She's cooking,' said Henry. 'She's

making about a million potato wedges
to use up the potatoes, she says.'

'Mine's chopping up salad,' said
Charlie, 'She says she's giving the
family a vitamin rush. And Dad's doing
something weird with coconuts in the
garden. What'll we do first? Make the
toast or decorate the street?'

'Decorate,' said Henry, and he
collected an armload of tinsel and
streamers while Charlie gathered up his
banner.

And then they went into the street together, and for the first time Charlie began to worry.

Their friendly street had never looked so empty.

There were no open doors.

No voices in gardens.

No people.

Even the cars were not in their familiar parking places. They were in an unfriendly huddle at the far end.

No dogs barked.

No cats prowled.

Even the rabbit hutches from Lulu's drive had gone.

It was a perfect blank.

A cold, uncomfortable feeling began in Charlie's stomach, but he did not say anything. He helped Henry drag a picnic table out into the street and they began decorating.

It was very, very hard to make Sellotape stick to lamp posts.

And the Christmas streamers streamed away in the breeze as if they wanted to escape.

The banner was a battle.

And the balloons would not blow up. Charlie and Henry blew and blew until they saw stars and went giddy, but the balloons stayed obstinately flat.

'I think that must be why we didn't use them at Christmas,' said Henry.

Charlie sighed and said, 'I'm going inside to make toast.'

They both felt better to be back in Henry's bedroom again. Charlie toasted and Henry spread marmite and they piled the slices on to two large plates, borrowed from the kitchen.

'Plenty of toast, anyway,' said Henry cheerfully. 'Let's take it out now. You bring the bananas! What about the curry?'

'What about it?' demanded Charlie, who since his encounter with the Yellow Car Man was feeling very protective about his curry.

'It doesn't look very nice, cold in a

bucket.'

'It won't be cold in a bucket when we give it to people,' snapped Charlie. 'It will be microwaved hot. On plates. I found a huge pile of paper plates in the kitchen this morning. I'll borrow those. I wish we had the apple pie. Old Mashed Potatoes is taking ages buying those candles.'

They left a space on the picnic table for the pie, put the toast next to the bucket, and arranged a fringe of bananas all round the edge.

'All Max's favourites,' said Henry, but somehow they did not look like Max's favourites.

The drooping decorations didn't look like decorations either.

And nothing could have looked more dismal than Charlie's dangling banner.

There was something wrong.

It didn't look like a party at all.

'I'll start playing my recorder when people begin coming,' said Henry. 'I hope that's soon.'

Then Charlie realized what was wrong, and what had given him the awful feeling in his stomach.

'Henry! Henry!' he cried. 'The invitations! They blew away!'

'Yes, but we picked them up,' said Henry.

'As many as we could. You took them home, didn't you?'

'Yes. But …'

'And you said I needn't bother making another set because you would sort them out.'

Charlie moaned.

Henry waited.

'I forgot,' said Charlie.

'You forgot?'

Charlie nodded.

'You didn't give invitations to anyone?'

Charlie shook his head.

'But,' said Henry, outraged, 'then no one will come!'

'No.'

'Or eat this toast!'

'No.'

'I've got thirty-one bananas here, Charlie!'

'Yes.'

'And I've been practising my recorder for ages and ages for this party!'

'I know.'

'But if you didn't give out any invitations, there won't be a party!'

'No.'

Henry sat down in the gutter and howled like a wolf. Charlie sat beside him with his head on his arms and for a long time he didn't speak and then at last he said, 'At least I didn't tell Max.'

'I did,' said Henry.

'What?'

'I did,' said Henry. 'This morning.

While he was taking photos. I said, "You'll have plenty to take pictures of this afternoon." And Max asked, "I will?" and I said, "Just be here at three o'clock, that's all. You'll get a surprise!" and Max said … Max said …'

Henry gulped.

'Max said, "I wouldn't miss it for anything".'

Then Henry put his head on his knees, and it was Charlie's turn to howl like a wolf.

Saturday afternoon.
Bash!

Charlie was still howling when the big boys came. Seven or eight of them from Max's class at school, led by Mike, Max's best friend, who lived further up the street.

'This the party then?' they demanded. 'The bash for Max? The big surprise? Those the decorations?' they asked. 'Great!' they said, and began unfurling streamers.

'Balloons!' they exclaimed, and *POOOFF* they blew and the balloons ballooned in seconds.

'String!' ordered Mike, and sent Charlie running.

Then the big boys got to work. They boosted each other up lamp posts and hung bunches of balloons. They strode along walls with tinsel in their teeth. They straightened up the banner and festooned the trees with streamers.

They piled presents on the table and set up three CD

players, all playing different tunes.

'How did you know to come?' asked Charlie, and Mike waved a blown-away invitation under his nose.

'Found it in the street,' he said.

Then Lulu came dancing out, a rabbit in one hand, forty-eight packets of crisps in the other. 'We've got to leave space for the lorry,' she announced. 'And Mum says we'll need more tables and can you fetch ours from round the back.'

'How did *you* know?' asked Charlie, and Lulu showed her own blown-away invitation. 'Darling Rocko, my big black dog, brought it home in his teeth,' she said proudly.

Another table appeared from Henry's house.

Coca-Cola.

Lemonade.

Cheesy dips.

And hot potato wedges.

Then more big boys with frisbees.

Remote control aeroplanes.

Skateboards.

Footballs.

And pic 'n' mix from the market.

A lorry arrived and, after much huffing and puffing, left a bouncy castle in Lulu's drive.

The girls came in a gang, laden with more streamers, more CD players, strawberries and giant pretend flowers.

'But where is Max?' they asked.

'Mike is in charge of Max,' said one of the big boys. 'He's got him back at his house. He's bringing him out at three.'

Sure enough, at three o'clock exactly, the front door of Mike's house was flung open and there was Max in his new hat and his sunglasses, grinning on the doorstep.

'SURPRISE!' yelled everyone.

'Hello, Max!' shouted Charlie.

'Gosh! Fantastic!' said Max. Then Mike pushed Max

out into the street, the girls gave him their flowers in a human-sized bouquet of pink daisies, and Henry said, 'What do you think? Did you guess? Look, thirty-one bananas! Have you got your camera?'

'Of course,' said Max, and took a photograph of Henry holding all thirty-one bananas.

And another of Charlie holding the
bunch of pink daisies.

And then the great big birthday bash
began.

Lulu put six rabbits on
the bouncy castle.

Charlie's mum
and dad
brought out a
coconut shy.

Hot dogs.

And a lot of
salad.

Old Mashed Potatoes came home
and found she had locked herself out.
The big boys hoisted Charlie up to
her bathroom window and he climbed

through and rescued the apple pie all by himself.

Doors opened all down the street, even the Yellow Car Man's door.

A football match began, mixed teams of humans and dogs. Lulu helped with the refereeing.

'Sit!' she cried, and half the players sat.

There were more people than Charlie could name, more things to eat than Charlie could count, more music than he could listen to, more games than he could ever have thought of. And yet people came up to him all the time saying, 'Well done, Charlie!'

'Nice one, Charlie!'

'Excellent, Charlie!'

'And Henry,' said Charlie, and added, 'he hasn't had a chance to play his recorder yet.'

The whole street went respectfully quiet while Henry stood on a chair and played 'Twinkle, Twinkle, Little Star' three times through with hardly any mistakes.

And at the end there were fireworks: twelve rockets because Max was twelve.

It was very, very late before Charlie went to bed. And even then he lay awake, remembering the best bits. The aeroplane race. The whole street rumba led by Henry on recorder with Max taking photographs, safe from the dancing. The arrival of the Yellow Car

Man carrying an enormous tray.

'Rice,' he had said, nodding at a dish. 'There's naan bread. Those are poppadoms. And *this* ... is *curry*!'

'Wow!' said Max.

'That's *not* curry,' said the Yellow Car Man, removing Charlie's bucket.

Later the Yellow Car Man had helped Max hoist Charlie and Henry on to a table to be cheered.

Max said, and everyone said, it had been the best party ever. The best birthday. The best bash.

So that was OK, thought Charlie, sleepily, but still, he couldn't help wondering, had it been a surprise?

Had Max been surprised?

Had any one of those dozens of people, turning up at exactly the right time with exactly the right things, been surprised?

Hmm, Charlie thought, yawning. Well. Maybe. Maybe not.

But ... I WAS SURPRISED!

WANT MORE CHARLIE?
READ MORE OF HIS ADVENTURES

in

CHARLIE
and the Cat Flap

1

Four Days Before the Big Sleep

Charlie and Henry were both seven years old, and they were best friends. They were best friends, and they quarrelled all the time. They argued at school. They squabbled at birthday parties.

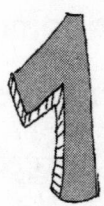

They nearly always had to be separated
on school trips. Their friends said,
'Charlie and Henry have been like that
for ever!' and took no notice; but their
teachers called them The Terrible Two.
'Double Trouble!' agreed Charlie and
Henry's fathers.

Their mothers said,

'You boys ALWAYS end up
quarrelling!'

One Monday morning, Charlie's big
brother Max asked if he could stay with
a friend for the night on Friday and
his mother said he could. This would
mean there would be an empty bed
in Charlie's bedroom. That Monday
afternoon, Charlie and Henry ran out
of school to where their mothers were

both standing moaning about them and Charlie asked, 'On Friday night, can Henry come for a sleepover?'

Straight away Charlie and Henry's mothers said,

'No!'

'No,' they said. 'We haven't forgotten the last time!'

The last time Henry's father had had to get dressed at two o'clock in the morning and take Charlie home because Charlie said he could not bear listening to the way Henry breathed for one moment longer.

'He is copying my breathing!' Charlie had complained furiously. 'Every time I breathe, he breathes! He has been doing it ever since you took away his

Super Soaker Water Squirter! And what has happened to my Itching Powder and my two dead flies? That's what I want to know!'

So Charlie had been taken home, and Henry's Super Soaker was banned for a week. But the Itching Powder and the two dead flies turned up safe and sound in Henry's bed, where Charlie had put them, and Charlie and Henry soon forgot all about their quarrel. They were astonished when their mothers reminded them. They looked at each other and they put on their Sad Little Boy faces and then they tried again.

Charlie said to his mother: 'You let Max have sleepovers but you won't let me!'

'You like Max better than me!'

'He's your favourite!'

'It's not fair!'

And Henry said to his mother: 'At least Charlie has Max! I have no brothers or sisters and I am fed up with living in a house just with grown-ups.'

Their mothers made moaning sounds but Charlie and Henry did not stop.

They said: 'We never quarrel!'

'Charlie likes it when I hit him.'

'Henry likes it when I push him over.'

'We only argue a bit.'

'I don't argue,' said Charlie.

'How can you say that?' asked Henry. 'You argue all the time!'

'Just because I don't agree with every single word you say!' said Charlie.

'Argue argue argue,' said Henry, sticking his thumbs in his ears and waving his fingers rudely at Charlie. 'Moan moan moan!'

'You think you are so clever!' said Charlie, grabbing at him. 'You are not half as clever as you think you are!'

'You are not a quarter as clever as you think you are,' replied Henry, dodging behind his mother.

'You are not a millionth!' shouted Charlie.

'You are not a quarter of a millionth!' said Henry.

Charlie was not very good at maths and he could not think of any amount smaller than a quarter of a millionth to say Henry was not as clever as, so he did not say anything. He stared up at the sky as if he did not care.

Henry came out from behind his

mother and stuck out his tongue to
show that he had won.

'Ha!' shouted Charlie, and jumped on
Henry and tipped him on to the ground.
It was always very easy for anyone to
tip Henry over. He did not seem to be

properly balanced.

Charlie sat down on top of Henry and Henry flung his arms about and bashed Charlie on the nose. It started to bleed at once. Charlie's nose always bled at the smallest bump. It did not seem to be very well made.

All this arguing and wrestling and nose bashing had taken less than two minutes.

And Charlie and Henry were still best friends at the end of it, but their mothers did not understand that.

MAMMOTH ACADEMY

Neal Layton's classic, lovable mammoths, Oscar and Arabella, are off to school and there's always trouble around the corner at The Mammoth Academy!